The Silent Man

By: Britt Wolfe

Copyright © 2025 Britt Wolfe

All rights reserved. No part of this book may be reproduced, distributed, or transmitted in any form or by any means, including (but not limited to) photocopying, recording, or telepathic osmosis, without prior written permission from the author.

This is a work of fiction. Any resemblance to actual persons, living or dead, is purely coincidental—unless you feel personally attacked, in which case, maybe do some self-reflection. The characters and events in this book are entirely products of the author's imagination, and any similarities to real life are either accidental or a sign that the simulation is glitching.

Cover design, formatting, and caffeine consumption by Britt Wolfe. Additional emotional support provided by Sophie and Lena.

First Edition: 2025

Printed in Canada because books deserve a solid passport stamp too.

For inquiries, praise, declarations of undying love, or to request permission for use beyond fair dealing (seriously, just ask first), please visit: BrittWolfe.com

If you enjoyed this book, please consider leaving a review. If you didn't, well, that's between you and your questionable taste.

This Novella Is Dedicated To:

My sister Andrea—for her quiet strength, her unshakeable resilience, and the way she has always led with grace and integrity, even when no one was watching. You taught me what it means to be steady in the storm. You are, and always have been, a light.

And to everyone who chooses courage over comfort.
To those who speak up.
Who stand up.
Who do what is right—not because it is easy or comfortable or convenient, but because it matters. Because it *always* matters.

This story is for the protectors.
For the truth-tellers.
For the brave hearts who choose action over apathy, love over loyalty to harm, and justice over the ease of looking away.

May your courage never go unnoticed.
This story is for you.
Because the world shifts when someone decides to stand.

The Silent Man
Is Inspired by: *The Smallest Man Who Ever Lived* by Taylor Swift

When I first heard The Smallest Man Who Ever Lived, I felt the sting of recognition. It's a song about romantic betrayal, yes—but beneath the heartbreak, there's something deeper. Something that speaks to the particular kind of devastation that comes not from strangers or enemies, but from those who were supposed to protect us. From the men who were given proximity, power, or permission to stand beside us—and instead stood by.

In The Silent Man, this story isn't about a romantic partner. It's about a father.

Because some of the most painful betrayals don't come from broken relationships, but from the roles that were never fulfilled to begin with. From the men who could have made a different choice and didn't. From the ones who let the harm happen while they turned their faces away, who failed to act, to speak, to save.

There might be other timelines out there—other versions of this story, other endings—where love won. Where truth was spoken. Where silence wasn't weaponized. Where girls were believed, defended, and held. But in this timeline? We only get the one life. And in this life, some choices are irreversible. Some damage is permanent. And some men never acknowledge what they did or didn't do—not even to themselves. They simply pass the blame and move on.

This novella is my reflection on that kind of damage in response to Taylor's incredible words. It's a deep dive into the pain of what could have been. And into the silent, staggering weight of being failed by the very people who should have stood up.

I hope this story finds the ones who were left to pick up the pieces.

Peace, Love, and Inspiration,

Britt Wolfe

The Silence That Echoed ~ Then

The house was glowing with soft lamplight, its warmth a lie told in amber. From the outside, it might have looked serene—domestic, even. Inside, the air was thick with heat and something more violent than anger: a coldness sharp enough to flay.

Aurora stood just inside the front door, the weight of her backpack a sudden, awkward presence slung low over one shoulder. Her fingers trembled at her side, nails bitten to the quick. She was careful not to exhale too loudly, not to shift too suddenly, as if the floor itself might betray her with a creak.

In the next room, Deanna's voice sliced through the evening like a shattered wine glass.

"I know it was you," she snapped, low and biting, like she'd been holding the sentence in her mouth all day, waiting for Aurora to arrive home. "Who else would be desperate enough to go through my purse?"

Aurora didn't respond. There was no point.

The kitchen light glared across the linoleum, too bright, too white. Deanna stood at the counter with a cigarette balanced between two fingers, her hair pulled back too tight, exposing the stark bones of her face. Her eyes gleamed with something feral, unblinking.

Graham sat at the table like a statue posed for silence. He didn't look up.

"I didn't take anything," Aurora said softly, though she knew her words were pointless.

Her voice was no match for the room, or the people in it—her own parents.

It hadn't been for years.

"Oh, sweetie, I'm not asking." Deanna took a drag from her cigarette and let out a bitter laugh. "You're fourteen, and already a thief. Just like your father's mother. All sharp edges and nothing to show for it."

Aurora's hands curled into fists inside her sleeves. She couldn't remember the last time her mother had said her name like it belonged to her, and not to a sin. Every word that left Deanna's mouth felt like a label being branded into her skin—thief, burden, liar. Nothing was said with love. Not to her.

Only to them. Her younger sisters.

Vanessa, seven years old and luminous with approval, sat at the end of the table, twirling a piece of hair around her finger, eyes gleaming with performative innocence. Her smile was subtle. Practiced.

Isla, five, said nothing at all. She never did. She sat like a shadow in the corner chair, hands in her lap, feet still not touching the floor.

Aurora was made of fire. Flaming red hair twisted into a loose braid, strands breaking free like they'd been born for rebellion. Her skin was the snowdrift-pale of girls who blistered under sunlight, kissed with freckles that ran like wildfire across her cheekbones–red, unruly, undeniable. Her aquamarine eyes—impossibly bright, startling—made strangers stop and stare. But not here. Not in her home. Here, she was a blemish. An echo of a mistake no one claimed.

She was beautiful.

She'd just never been told.

"Don't look at me like that," Deanna snapped, pushing off the counter and moving toward her eldest daughter with the grace of a storm. "Like you're innocent. Like you're some fragile little doll. You're not. You're trouble, and you know it."

Aurora blinked slowly, unwilling to let the tears fall. She looked to her father, still sitting placidly at the kitchen table—then to her mother, and back again. Her gaze settled on him, pleading, willing him to say something. Do something.

But he just sat there.

"It wasn't me," Aurora said again, softer this time, the protest barely a breath. She hoped the tremble in her voice didn't betray her, but it was too late. No one was coming to save her. Not here. Not ever. She would have to be her own protector—again.

Deanna's hand was sudden, sharp—a flash of motion across the soft glow of the room. The slap wasn't hard enough to bruise, but it was cruel enough to leave a sting behind. Not just on the skin. In the marrow.

Graham still didn't move.

Not a word. Not a flinch. Not even the tremor of a breath.

"Go on," Deanna said, stepping back. "Get out. You want to steal? You want to act like you don't belong here? Fine. You don't." Deanna gestured toward the door Aurora had walked through just moments ago.

Vanessa's eyes sparkled, unbothered. Isla blinked once, her lip trembling, but she looked away.

Aurora turned to her father. She didn't speak. She just looked.

There was nothing she could say that would reach him now, but she willed him to say something. To stand up for her. To protect her. To do anything.

Her gaze was a question.

His silence was the answer.

He sat with one hand still resting on his coffee cup, steam curling upward like smoke from a fire long burned out. He was always drinking coffee late into the night.

Not a flicker of defence.

Not even the soft grace of pity.

Only absence, dressed up in a father's body.

Aurora turned.

The hallway behind her stretched out like a tunnel she'd already walked through a hundred times in her dreams. The pictures on the wall—baby photos of Vanessa, Isla's crooked smile, one faded school portrait of Aurora from grade two—felt like a cruel joke now. The smell of lemon cleaner and something scorched lingered in the air.

She walked to her bedroom. Quiet. Controlled. She didn't slam the door. She didn't cry.

The pale blue walls were covered in curling band posters. A few bracelets she never wore anymore were draped over the mirror. There was a half-finished art project on the desk—a cityscape in charcoal, all hard edges and vanishing points. No colour. She picked up her backpack and filled it with what mattered.

Not much did.

A hoodie. A Walkman. Lip balm. A copy of *Catcher in the Rye* with a broken spine.

The light through the window had softened now—pink and peach washing over the rooftops outside, the kind of light that makes even ugly places look almost holy.

Aurora had to walk back through the kitchen to leave through the front door. Her mother wasn't there anymore when she did. Graham and Vanessa had started playing a boardgame. Neither looked up as she walked by.

Isla met her near the front door. Her large eyes watching behind soupy tears threatening to spill. Aurora looked at her youngest sister, smiled, then looked away before tears came to her own eyes.

She paused on the porch for just a moment. The front door clicked shut behind her, the sound definitive. The breeze lifted a strand of hair and pushed it across her cheek. Her bare arms prickled.

The street was empty. The whole world felt paused and lonely.

She looked back at the house that had been her home for fourteen years, one final time, hoping—aching—for the door to creak open.

For Graham to step outside.

For someone to call her name.

For someone to tell her to come back inside.

Nothing.

The window above the sink glowed amber.

Then the curtains were drawn.

And that, she thought, was the loudest thing of all.

So she turned. And she walked.

Away from the house that never loved her.

Away from the silence that never broke.

And into the night that would.

Part I
The Past They Lived

The Aftermath ~ Isla Present Day

The house was too quiet for a day like this.

No casserole dishes. No visitors with low, pitying voices and hands that hovered near her elbow. No flowers in cellophane wrapping, their scent already beginning to rot. Just silence.

The kind that sat heavy in the walls and settled deep in your bones.

Isla moved through it like she wasn't sure she belonged in the moment. Like it might collapse if she stepped too loudly.

Her mother was dead.

She was back in the house where she had been raised.

And the house had stayed exactly the same.

The hallway still creaked in the same spots. The baseboard near the front door still had the crack from where Deanna had kicked it one winter afternoon—Aurora had said something unforgivable, or nothing at all, and the door hadn't slammed fast enough behind her. Isla couldn't remember the details. Only the sound.

Even now, years later, the sound still echoed.

She sat in the armchair in the front room, legs curled beneath her, fingers wrapped around a mug she hadn't yet remembered to drink from. She stared at nothing. At everything.

The television was off.

The light through the blinds striped across the carpet like prison bars.

The scent of lemon polish still clung to the air, but faintly. Like memory. Like it had been trying to leave for years and didn't know how.

Her mother had died in the upstairs bedroom just before dawn. Alone. Isla had stayed through the night, sitting downstairs with the door cracked open, waiting for something she couldn't name.

She didn't cry.

She hadn't cried yet.

She wasn't sure if she would.

Graham was in the kitchen, silent as always. He'd washed the coffee pot that morning. Quietly. Methodically. She'd heard the sound of ceramic mugs clinking, the soft shuffle of his slippers. As if nothing had changed. As if the woman who had filled every corner of this house with rage and ritual and noise had not just vanished from the world.

She didn't know if he was grieving. Or if he even knew how. She didn't really know him at all.

Maybe he'd mourned Deanna in pieces, over decades. Or maybe he'd buried everything so deep that he couldn't access it even now. Maybe he'd stopped loving her years ago. Maybe he'd never started.

Isla didn't ask. It didn't matter now.

She didn't know how to speak to her father. Not really. They shared space like ghosts passing through walls. The last time they'd had a conversation longer than two sentences, she'd still been in university. Before everything fractured and became even more of a wreckage.

Before Vanessa made it impossible. Made everything impossible.

Vanessa.

God, even just thinking her name made Isla's chest tighten.

Of course she wasn't here.

Of course the lawyer had already called.

She was *contesting the will.*

Isla could hear her voice now—sharp, cool, calculated. The same way she'd always been when she wanted something. Like charm painted over arsenic.

"I just think it's suspicious," she'd said on the voicemail, barely thirty seconds after the time of death. "Mom would never leave anything to Isla. That's not even logical."

Logical.

As if logic had ever lived in this house.

Isla hadn't responded. She didn't need to. Vanessa would escalate anyway. It was her nature.

For her, grief was a transaction. A stage. A chess game. And the board was already in play.

The front steps creaked—a sound Isla had memorized as a child, waiting in her bed to know who was home and what kind of night it would be.

This time it was just the wind.

She sipped from the mug finally. Cold percolator coffee. Bitter.

Outside, the day was still soft and pale. Spring hadn't quite arrived, but there was a hint of thaw. The snow was crusted grey along the edges of the lawn, and the trees stood like bare-armed sentinels. The sky was a dull sheet of pewter, the kind that promised rain but rarely delivered it. The kind that never quite wept.

She rested her cheek against the arm of the chair and closed her eyes.

Somewhere in her chest, a weight pulsed.

She couldn't name it, exactly.

Relief?

Sadness?

Emptiness?

Was it wrong to feel lightness in the wake of death? Not joy. But something like... oxygen. Like the air had shifted, just slightly, and the world wasn't holding its breath anymore.

The grief wasn't for Deanna.

It was for the childhood Isla had never been given. For the softness she had watched in other families and longed for like something mythical. For the way Graham had lit up around Vanessa only. For the door that closed behind Aurora and never opened again.

She didn't remember much about the day her oldest sister left. Just that the house felt colder after. More dangerous in its quiet.

Deanna had only gotten meaner after that.

And Graham had only grown quieter, more ambivalent.

The clock on the wall ticked. Steady. Impersonal.

Isla sat with her knees tucked beneath her, in the house where everything had happened, waiting for something inside her to shatter.

But there was no shattering.

Only the strange, weightless knowledge that her mother was gone.

And now, maybe—*finally*—the story could begin again.

The Return ~ Aurora Present Day

She almost didn't answer the phone.

It was a blocked number, and Aurora had learned long ago that nothing good came from unexpected calls. But something—intuition, or maybe just a sick kind of curiosity—made her tap to accept.

She stood in the middle of a sunlit kitchen two hundred kilometres from anywhere that mattered, barefoot on cold tile, the sound of the lawyer's voice carrying through the static like it belonged to another life.

Her mother was dead.

The news landed not like a punch, but like a silence. Vast. Bottomless. The kind of silence that makes your ears ring. The kind that says, You're not done with this yet.

She hung up without saying much. Just "okay." Just "thanks."

And then she stood there for a long time, staring out the window at the neighbour's laundry flapping in the breeze. A pair of pink bedsheets danced on the line like they didn't know the world had shifted.

She hadn't been back in fourteen years.

Not once.

Not after the night she walked down that cracked street, heart hammering in her ribs, waiting for the front door to open. For someone to call out after her. It never did.

Aurora Lockwood had built an entire life on that moment. On the silence that followed.

And now, they wanted her to come back. To the house where she was unmade. To the man who watched it happen. To the ghost of sisters she didn't know.

She drove in the rain.

Not because she wanted to, but because she had to see it for herself. The death. The survival. The wreckage left behind.

The highway stretched long and empty, the trees on either side bowed under the weight of late March damp. Her windshield wipers worked hard against the downpour, and still, her vision blurred at the edges. Not with tears. With memory.

The closer she got to Jim Thorpe, the smaller she felt.

Like her body remembered the version of her that never belonged.

Like the land itself could see through the tattoos and the cigarette habit and the low, steady voice she'd taught herself to use in boardrooms and back alleys.

The house appeared slowly, like something summoned.

Same sagging porch. Same lopsided fence post. The front yard was more patchwork than lawn—snow clinging to the shadows, the ground beneath it thawing into mud. Her boots sank half an inch when she stepped out of the car.

She stood there for a moment, one hand still resting on the car door, the other curled tightly around her keys.

She hadn't told Isla she was coming.

She didn't know what she'd say if she did.

It was Isla that stopped her in the hallway that last night. The way the girl turned her face, lip trembling, too scared to speak. Five years old. Already learning how to disappear.

Aurora had carried that memory like a splinter beneath her skin.

The front steps creaked beneath her weight. The wood was soft now, rotted at the edges.

When she knocked, the sound felt sacrilegious.

The door opened slowly.

And there she was.

Isla Lockwood.

Older, of course. Her hair was longer. Her face thinner. But the eyes were the same. Wide and dark, still heavy with quiet.

They stared at each other.

Neither of them spoke.

Then, Isla stepped aside.

Aurora walked in.

The house hadn't changed.

It hit her like a slap. The lemon cleaner. The pale wallpaper, peeling now at the edges. The hook by the door where Deanna used to hang her purse like a trophy.

The couch was different. But the layout was the same. The air was the same. Still stale with a grief that never aired out.

She walked down the hall like someone retracing a crime scene.

When she reached her old bedroom, she paused in the doorway.

No one had touched it.

Not really.

The posters had long been stripped from the walls, but the pinholes remained. The closet door still had the crack in the mirror from when she'd kicked it at thirteen, crying so hard her teeth rattled. The windowsill still bore the burn mark from a candle she wasn't supposed to have.

Dust lay thick on every surface. The bed had no sheets.

It was a room frozen in time.

A room abandoned by everyone but the house.

She stepped inside.

It smelled like old paper and forgotten things. The closet door groaned when she nudged it open. On the top shelf, she spotted a box—plain, unlabelled, covered in a fine film of years.

She pulled it down. Set it on the bed.

Inside: a few drawings, crumpled and faded. A hair elastic. A t-shirt from a school she barely remembered. Nothing valuable. Nothing worth keeping.

But someone had kept it anyway.

She sank onto the mattress. It creaked beneath her, like it remembered her too.

Her fingers grazed the windowsill, where she used to sit late at night, knees tucked to her chest, counting the cars that passed, pretending they were coming for her. That someone would stop. Would knock. Would see her.

"I didn't know if you'd come," Isla's voice was soft, from the doorway.

Aurora didn't turn.

"I didn't either," she said.

A beat of silence.

"I didn't think I'd ever see you again," Aurora said, softer now.

Blood and Bruises ~ Isla Age Ten

The air in the house had its own texture that day.

Heavy. Close. Like the whole place was holding its breath.

It was a Sunday—one of those bright, brittle winter mornings where the snow outside made everything inside feel too quiet, like sound didn't travel properly. The heat clicked through the vents in short, impatient bursts. Somewhere down the hall, the dryer hummed, turning and turning.

Isla stood at the kitchen counter, arms locked stiffly at her sides. A mixing bowl sat in front of her. Flour clung to her sweater. She was wearing her best one—the pale blue with the silver thread in the collar. Her mother liked this one. Said it made her look less washed out and took attention away from her too-large forehead.

She'd tried to braid her own hair that morning, copying the way Vanessa did hers—tight, precise, glossy. Isla's braid was none of those things. It was fine and flyaway, full of static, one side already slipping loose where her fingers had trembled too much.

Deanna had said nothing about the braid. Only frowned when Isla added too much sugar to the bowl.

"I said level," her mother muttered, grabbing the measuring cup from her hands with a sharp tug. "You can't even follow *simple instructions*."

"I'm sorry," Isla said.

She said it the way other people said *hello*. Like punctuation.

From the table, Vanessa sighed loudly. She was twelve now, legs crossed, flipping through a magazine she didn't really need to read. Her hair gleamed like varnished wood, twisted up into a clip she'd stolen from a girl at school. She didn't look up when she spoke.

"She always ruins things."

Isla flinched. Not visibly, she hoped.

Deanna snorted softly and poured the sugar back into the canister, muttering under her breath. Something about incompetence. About not having the energy to start over.

Isla didn't move.

She didn't breathe too loud.

She didn't cry.

Crying made everything worse.

Across the room, Graham stood by the sink, nursing a mug of coffee. He wasn't reading the book in his hand. He wasn't even pretending. He was just watching. Not closely. Not in the way you watch when you *see*.

Just... existing in his usual state of aloof ambivalence.

His silence was the furniture in this house—always present, never questioned.

Vanessa turned the page of her magazine and sighed again, this time louder. "I don't know why you let her help, Mom. She can't do anything right."

"I just wanted to try," Isla whispered.

Vanessa looked up slowly. Smiled sweetly. "Oh, I know," she said. "You're always trying."

There was something sharp in her voice, so thin it barely registered unless you'd lived inside it long enough to feel the edge. Isla had. She knew that tone better than her own.

"You can go set the table," Deanna said flatly to Isla, not looking up.

Isla nodded, grateful for the task. She grabbed the plates with both hands, careful not to clink them too loudly as she moved. Noise was unpredictable. Noise could become something.

At the table, Vanessa stuck her foot out. Just enough.

Isla tripped.

The plates didn't fall. Not all of them. One landed on the edge of the table and spun before crashing to the floor, a perfect, awful shatter.

The sound was enormous.

Deanna spun around. "*Jesus*, Isla!"

"I—I tripped—"

"Of course you did." Denna's voice dripped with disdain and disbelief.

"I didn't mean to—Vanessa—"Isla stammered.

"Don't blame your sister." Isla looked at Graham. He hadn't moved, but suddenly he could speak.

Vanessa sat at the table, chin in hand, eyes wide with faux surprise. "I didn't touch her," she said softly.

Her tone was syrupy. Unbothered. Practiced.

Deanna turned back to the mess and waved a dismissive hand.

"Clean that up," she snapped. "And go to bed."

Isla's face burned as she crouched down, gathering sharp pieces of porcelain with hands that wouldn't stop shaking.

She didn't say anything else.

When she was finished, she locked herself in the upstairs bathroom, pulled her sleeves up, and stared at the mark blooming beneath her elbow. A perfect fingerprint-shaped bruise. Vanessa's hand. From earlier, when she'd grabbed her arm too hard during a "game." Just a joke. Just teasing.

Just a lie.

Isla traced the bruise with one finger. She didn't cry.

She listened to her family downstairs eating dinner without her. Heard Vanessa announce there would be no dessert because Isla had ruined it.

Isla crept downstairs later and found her father in the den, watching a hockey game he didn't care about. He didn't look away from the screen when she sat beside him.

"Dad?" she said, softly.

He blinked. "Yeah?"

She rolled up her sleeve.

The bruise looked even worse now, spreading like a flower.

"She hurts me," Isla said quietly. "Vanessa."

Graham looked at the bruise. Not for long.

He didn't react.

He didn't ask questions.

He took a sip of his beer and let out a long, tired breath.

"Don't cause drama, Isla," he said dismissively.

Her stomach dropped.

"She does it when no one's looking," she tried. "She lies about it. And Mom—she always believes her—"

Graham held up a hand. Not angry. Just... ambivalent, avoidant, tired.

"Just stay out of her way," he said. "You know how she is."

Isla opened her mouth.

Closed it again.

And that was that.

She went back upstairs and didn't speak of it again.

Not to him. Not to anyone.

The bruise faded.

The silence didn't.

And the worst part was—Isla didn't know which hurt more.

The Favourite ~ Vanessa Present Day

Grief didn't suit her, but she wore it anyway. Like a string of pearls draped carefully over a silk blouse—an accessory more than a truth.

Vanessa Lockwood sat at the head of the conference table in the law office, ankles crossed neatly beneath her chair, fingers steepled just under her chin. Her blazer was the colour of mourning, but her lipstick was perfect, and her voice—when she finally chose to use it—was as smooth and sharp as a polished blade.

"I'm not here to cause problems," she said, smiling just enough to be disarming. "I'm here to correct an oversight."

The lawyer, some freckled man with thinning hair and ill-fitting sleeves, shifted in his seat. "Miss Lockwood, your mother's will was witnessed and signed in accordance with state law—"

"My mother was on fentanyl," Vanessa interrupted sweetly with her baseless and impossible lie. "Let's not pretend this was a woman operating at full capacity. Or memory. Or fairness."

A pause. Calculated.

"I loved her," she added, just in case the room was too cold for sympathy.

And she did. In the way you love a storm—until you realize it's not one storm, but two. Until the wind changes, and it's not your mother's cruelty this time, but your own. Worse. Sharper. More piercing and violent.

Like Deanna passed the torch and Vanessa said, *watch this*.

She had once been closest to Deanna in a way.

Not out of affection, but alignment. They were allies, once—co-conspirators in cruelty, twin storms twisting through the house. But alliances like that never last. Not when both want control. Not when pain is currency. By thirteen, the bond had splintered into something volatile. One fight too loud, one shove too hard—Vanessa at the top of the stairs, Deanna at the bottom, watching her fall.

And Graham… well. Graham adored Vanessa. Always had.

Vanessa had felt it since childhood. The subtle shift in his tone when he spoke her name. The pride in his eyes when she did anything—when she performed, when she didn't. The softness he reserved only for her. Vanessa had never had to beg for her father's love. It had been planted in her hands like a promise.

She'd protected it.

She hadn't earned it. Though she believed she did.

She told herself she'd held the house together when Isla cracked at the edges and Aurora disappeared like smoke. That she'd brought order. That she'd silenced chaos. But she hadn't done a thing. She'd simply stayed—entitled, idle, handed everything by a father too blind to see what she was becoming. She didn't work. She didn't contribute. But in her mind, she was the backbone, the saviour, the one who'd earned it all. She had nothing to show for it—except her certainty that she deserved everything.

So no—Vanessa didn't feel guilt. She didn't mourn.

She felt *entitlement*.

To her, the will had been a slap in the face. A betrayal dressed in paperwork and witnessed signatures. As if Isla—quiet, spineless Isla—was the daughter who deserved to carry Deanna's name forward. As if she hadn't spent the better part of her life lurking in the corners of the family like a water stain.

Isla, the delicate one. Isla, the silent.

Isla, the inheritance.

Vanessa's fingers tapped once, lightly, against the glass of water the assistant had brought her. She didn't drink it.

Later, in the back of a cab, Vanessa pulled her phone from the fraying reusable bag she'd grabbed at a dollar store years ago. Not a purse. Not even a handbag. Just a faded, overused tote that had never been meant to last this long. She stared at the screen for a long time. One new message from Isla. Two lines.

Please don't do this. We could figure something out together.

Vanessa smiled to herself, satisfied to be back under her younger sister's skin.

Together. That word had always sounded cheap coming from Isla's mouth. As if they'd ever been equals. As if Vanessa hadn't spent their entire childhood having to correct Isla.

She opened the message again. Let her eyes skim it once more.

Then deleted it without a second thought.

She leaned back against the headrest, staring out the window as Jim Thorpe slid past—blurry and wet and full of people who didn't know a thing about loyalty.

Isla remembered bruises.

Vanessa remembered weakness.

There had always been something dangerous about Isla's softness. That kind of vulnerability invited chaos. Invited pity. Invited rescue. Vanessa had tried to harden her. Tried to prepare her for a world that would eat her alive.

Sometimes that meant being harsh.

Sometimes that meant pushing her. Grabbing too tightly. Speaking too sharply. Reminding her where she stood.

She never hit her. Not really. She taught her. And there was a difference.

She wasn't cruel. She was corrective.

Even now, she didn't think of it as abuse. No—Vanessa saw herself as the one who had stepped up when no one else would. She was the one who set the rules. Who held the line. She was the one who did the work no one appreciated.

It was parenting, in the absence of anyone else willing to do the damn job.

And Isla? Isla was still too soft to say thank you.

Vanessa had been seven when Aurora left. Isla had still been in pigtails and picture books. Their mother had crumpled inward in the months that followed, and Graham had buried himself in routine. It had fallen to Vanessa to keep the machine running.

And she had.

Now Isla wanted to rewrite history. Claim victimhood like it was an inheritance too.

But Vanessa remembered Isla skipping school and hiding letters from the counsellor. She remembered Isla lying about anxiety and "not feeling safe." It was attention-seeking. And manipulative. And ungrateful.

But now, according to the will, Isla was the golden one. The one deserving of a heirloom ring.

And Vanessa?

Vanessa was the villain.

She reached into her bag and pulled out her sunglasses, sliding them into place with a practiced hand.

She wasn't going to lose.

Not to Isla.

Not to Aurora, who had abandoned all of them and somehow still returned, probably for sympathy.

Not to her father's empty grief, or the ghost of Deanna, or a system that couldn't begin to understand the architecture of loyalty.

She was the one who stayed.

And she would be the one left standing.

Scar Sisters ~ Aurora and Isla Present Day

The house still creaked with the kind of weighted silence that only happens after death. Not just the loss of a person—but the unraveling of the force that held all the shadows in place.

Isla stood on the threshold of the porch with a blanket draped over her shoulders, a chipped mug of something lukewarm in her hands. She hadn't realized Aurora had come out too—until she caught a glimpse of that unmistakable red hair, vivid even in the dark, lit gold by the low porch light.

Aurora was perched on the top step, a cigarette pinched between two fingers, its ember pulsing like a heartbeat. Her boots were off, one leg pulled up, her chin resting on her knee.

Neither of them spoke at first.

There was too much history to cut through quickly. Too much silence stretched thin between them like an old thread—frayed, but unbroken.

Isla lowered herself onto the porch swing with the kind of quietness that came from practice. The blanket fell across her knees. Her mug steamed faintly. They sat like that for a long while, the space between them filled with the hum of streetlights, the rustle of tree branches, and the distant sound of a dog barking somewhere down the road.

"I always hated this porch," Aurora said, finally. Her voice was rough around the edges. "Too many goodbyes happened here."

Isla let out a breath. "It feels different now."

"Everything does," Aurora replied.

Isla looked at her. Really looked.

Aurora was still striking. Still all sharp angles and impossible contrast—snow-pale skin, that flame-red hair, freckles like stars, and those aquamarine eyes that could cut through rooms without even trying. She looked older, grown-up. Built. Like someone who had survived things that didn't want to be survived.

Isla didn't know what to say. She wrapped the blanket tighter around herself.

"I didn't think you'd come," she finally managed, but only softly.

Aurora shrugged. "I didn't think you'd want me to."

Another long pause stretched between them.

"I didn't know what to believe," Isla admitted, her voice barely above the hush of the wind. "They said so many things about you. That you were trouble. That you wanted to leave. That you didn't care about anyone but yourself."

Aurora didn't flinch. She took a slow drag from her cigarette and exhaled through her nose.

"They made sure of that," she said, almost gently. "Mom knew what she was doing. They needed someone to blame for the cracks."

Isla looked down at her mug.

"I was five," she whispered. "And you were fourteen. And in my head, that felt like... I don't know. Like you were grown. Like you could handle it."

Aurora turned her head then. "But I wasn't."

"I know that now," Isla said. "God, Aurora. I'm twenty-seven. I meet fourteen-year-olds at work and they're just... babies. And mom and dad let you walk out the front door like it was nothing."

Aurora's expression didn't change. But her fingers twitched against her knee. "I didn't go willingly," she said quietly. "They pushed me."

The words sat between them like a bruise.

"I'm sorry," Isla said, eyes stinging. "I should have... I don't know. Spoken up. Fought for you."

"You were five," Aurora said. "And I was a story someone else told you."

They sat with that truth for a while.

The night stretched long and silver-blue around them, a sky full of quiet stars, the air beginning to carry the edge of spring.

"I used to imagine what you were doing," Isla said after a while. "After you left. I thought maybe you lived in some cool apartment in Philadelphia. That you had red lipstick and leather boots and people who knew you were fascinating."

Aurora gave a huff of something like a laugh. "Try a shelter in Reading and three different schools before dropping out at sixteen."

Isla looked over at her, pain flickering in her expression. "I didn't know," she whispered.

"No one did," Aurora said. "That was the point."

The swing rocked gently beneath Isla, wood groaning in protest.

"I thought Vanessa was good," she said suddenly, bitterly. "She told me she was protecting me. That you were the one hurting me. And I believed her."

"She learned from the best," Aurora murmured. "Mom taught her how to twist love into something you had to earn."

Isla looked away. "I didn't know what love looked like."

"I didn't either," Aurora said. "Not until I left. Not until I stopped expecting it to come from this house."

A silence opened between them—this one softer.

Isla drew in a breath. "Do you remember the plum tree in the backyard?"

Aurora smiled faintly. "That crooked thing that only grew two sad plums a year?"

"I used to sit under it when they fought," Isla said. "I'd count the blossoms and pretend I lived somewhere else. I didn't know you used to do the same thing."

"I didn't," Aurora said, flicking ash from the edge of the porch. "I used to sit in the bathroom with the fan on and write letters I never sent. To imaginary family who cared."

Isla blinked. "What did they say?"

Aurora didn't answer right away.

Then, quietly: "They said I missed someone I never got to know."

Isla wiped at her eyes. "God, Aurora. We missed everything, didn't we?"

"Not everything," Aurora said. "We're here."

They sat in silence again, but this time it wasn't the kind that hurt.

It was the kind that healed.

They shared stories then. Small ones. Ridiculous ones. About the time Isla dropped her popsicle in Deanna's shoes left out on the porch and blamed it on the neighbour's kid. About how Aurora once poured glitter in Vanessa's shampoo bottle and denied it so hard even *she* started to believe herself.

They laughed—quietly, hesitantly at first, then louder. Laughter that sounded like freedom. Like old echoes finding their way home.

The stars moved overhead.

Eventually, the cigarette burned out, and Isla's drink went cold.

Aurora turned to her and said, "It wasn't your fault. You were just trying to survive."

"So were you," Isla replied.

They didn't hug.

They didn't need to.

The porch swing kept creaking, and the wind kept blowing, and somewhere in the bones of the house, a door closed forever.

But out here—on this porch, on this night—they began again.

Not as enemies. Not as ghosts.

But as girls who had bled in the same house, and somehow, still lived to tell it.

Scar sisters.

Threaded together by pain.

Bound now by something gentler.

Part II
The Life That Should Have Been

What Might Have Been ~ An Alternate Timeline

There are moments in a life that look like nothing.

Barely a blink. A breath. A choice so small it barely rustles the fabric of the day.

Moments that pass unnoticed as they flit by—but years later, decades later, they show their teeth. You look back and realize everything came down to that. One word not said. One step not taken. One breath held too long.

Graham Lockwood had one of those moments.

Really, his life was stitched together by moments like that—because his entire personality was built on laziness, and the quiet art of doing absolutely nothing while feeling entitled to absolutely everything.

It wasn't dramatic. There was no thunder. No divine warning or fateful omen. It was a Thursday, or maybe a Tuesday—he could never quite remember—and the kitchen smelled like garlic and scorched tomato sauce. Aurora was standing near the fridge with her arms folded tightly across her chest, her shoulders drawn up like she was preparing to be hit. Not with a hand. With words. With the kind that left invisible bruises. The kind that rearranged who you thought you were.

Deanna was mid-tirade. Sharp. Precise. Tearing into their eldest daughter with the same surgical cruelty she always wielded when she needed to feel bigger than the room.

And Graham—

He was sitting at the kitchen table.

Frozen.

Not because he agreed with his wife.

Not because he didn't care.

Because silence required nothing. Because conflict meant effort. Because doing the right thing took more energy than he was ever willing to give. Over the years, he hadn't just learned how to disappear inside his own skin—he'd mastered it. Made an art of apathy.

He knew the way Deanna treated their eldest and youngest daughters was wrong. He knew it early, and often, and clearly. But still, he did nothing—comforting himself with the idea that restraint was righteousness. That not participating made him clean. All his life, he'd thought of himself as a good man, despite every quote he'd ever read about evil thriving where good men do nothing. He'd simply decided he wasn't the one they were talking about.

It should have been nothing. A typical evening. One of many.

But in that moment, the world split.

In one version of the story—the version that would become their reality—Graham stayed seated. He watched. He waited. He turned his face to his coffee, the one always in his hand at all hours of every day, and let the storm pass, as he always had. And in that silence, Aurora left the house. Left the family. Left the version of herself she might have been.

But what if—

What if he had stood up?

What if, just once, he had placed his body between her and the blow?

What if he had spoken?

What if he had said enough?

This is the other version.

The parallel thread.

The door the Lockwoods could have walked through had he turned the knob.

The timeline no one got to live—but that still hums, quietly, beneath the one that was.

The life that could have bloomed from a moment of—not even bravery—just the kindness a child should never have to earn from their parent.

The story that would have begun with a single, simple act:
He stood.
He spoke.
She stayed.

Glimpses Of Light ~ An Alternate Timeline

It begins in the kitchen, because of course it does.

The light is the same as it always is at that time of evening—thin and colourless, bleeding in through the narrow window above the sink in wan streaks. It turns everything greyer, even the yellow walls that Deanna insisted on painting herself the summer Isla turned five. The paint never quite covered the old colour. It was patchy near the corners, a little uneven along the baseboards. It didn't matter. No one mentioned it again.

The floor is clean, but only just. The linoleum, once white, has yellowed from years of salt-stained boots and spilled juice and Deanna's harsh hands dragging the mop in angry, circular bursts.

The house smells like garlic and soap and something bitter cooking too fast. The air is close, like it's holding something. Like it knows what's coming.

Aurora stands near the fridge. Her hair is wild today—she didn't brush it. Red curls pulled into a messy braid that's already slipping loose, strands clinging to her freckled cheeks. She's too pale, as always. Her eyes are impossibly bright and wide, her shoulders hunched, her hands jammed into the sleeves of her oversized sweatshirt. She's fourteen and made of edges. She's trying not to show her fear. She's trying to shrink and to burn at the same time.

It's not the same night she left, but it's a similar evening from before. One of the many nights that led to the leaving.

Deanna is at the stove. Cigarette in hand, voice sharp enough to cut bone.

"You're just like your grandmother," she says, loud enough that the words echo. "Always sulking, always walking around like the world owes you something. You think I don't see what you're doing? You think you're clever?"

Aurora doesn't speak.

Her silence is a wall. It is also an offering.

Deanna turns, jabbering her cigarette at her like it's a weapon. "I asked you a question."

Nothing.

Deanna's voice climbs. "Don't you *dare* ignore me. You come into this house late, looking like a tramp, and now you're going to pretend you don't hear me?"

There's a brief flicker behind Aurora's eyes—pain, or rage, or something between them. Her mouth twitches, opens a fraction. She stops herself before arguing the insult. A *tramp?* In this? A baggy, oversized sweatshirt with Mickey Mouse on the front?

"Don't," Deanna snaps. "Whatever bullshit excuse you're about to pull out of that smug mouth, save it."

So Aurora says nothing. The quiet between them is brittle. Radiant. About to shatter.

And then—

Graham breathes.

That's all.

He breathes. Pushes his chair back from the kitchen table with a soft scrape. The motion is so small, so unfamiliar, that both Aurora and Deanna freeze.

He hasn't moved in years, not like this.

He rises slowly.

He's still in his work clothes—creased slacks, a navy sweater with a faint smear across the sleeve from where Isla had hugged him earlier with peanut butter fingers. His hair is slightly mussed. His face is unreadable. But he's *standing*.

The room tilts.

Deanna narrows her eyes. "What are you doing?"

Graham doesn't answer right away. He walks to the counter. Picks up a towel. Wipes his hands on it. Folds it slowly, precisely, like the moment needs that kind of reverence.

Then he turns.

He speaks, voice quiet, calm, *steady*, "that's enough."

The words fall like marbles onto the floor—small, solid, undeniable.

Deanna blinks. "Excuse me?"

He meets her eyes.

And this time, he doesn't look away.

"She didn't do anything wrong," he says.

"She—"

"I said," he repeats, "she didn't do anything wrong. And even if she had, this isn't how we handle it."

His voice doesn't rise.

It doesn't need to.

Deanna's nostrils flare. "So you're going to start playing dad now?"

"I've *always* been her dad," he replies. "I just didn't act like it. And that's going to change."

The air shifts.

You can feel it. Like a barometer drop before a storm. Like something in the bones of the house is loosening for the first time in years.

Deanna laughs once, short and sharp and too loud.

She turns back to the stove. "Well, look at you. Man of the hour."

He doesn't respond.

He doesn't need to.

Because Aurora is still standing near the fridge, but her posture has changed. Slightly. Just a fraction. Her shoulders have uncurled. Her hands have emerged from the sleeves of her sweatshirt. Her mouth is still drawn, but not tight.

She's watching him.

Not with hope, exactly.

But with *possibility*.

And that's something.

Later that evening, after Deanna has clanged the dishes into the sink and gone upstairs to run a bath that will last too long and echo down the hall, Graham finds Aurora in the living room.

She's sitting on the floor, her back against the wall, headphones draped around her neck. Her eyes are puffy. Her nose is red. She's pretending to read, but the book is upside down.

He doesn't say anything.

He just lowers himself onto the floor beside her. Not too close. Just enough.

She doesn't look up.

After a minute, he says, "I should've said something sooner."

She shrugs. "Doesn't matter."

"It does," he says. "You've been carrying it alone. You're 14. You're a child."

Still she doesn't look at him.

He watches the book in her hands. The worn edges. The tiny trembling movement of her thumbs.

"I'm not going to let her talk to you like that again," he says.

A beat.

Then, quietly, so softly he almost misses it: "You really mean that?"

He turns his head. Meets her eyes.

"Yes."

She nods, once, and looks away quickly, like she's afraid he'll see the emotion she hasn't allowed herself to feel in years.

He doesn't push.

He just sits with her.

And in that quiet, for the first time in a long time, she begins to believe someone might actually stand for her—here, in these fragile years when she's still too small to stand for herself, too unarmed to face the mother who brought her into the world as the very enemy she needed protection from.

The house felt different the next morning.

Not in any obvious way. No great shift. No apologies left on the table. No hugs or heart-to-hearts.

But the air felt lighter. Like someone had finally opened a window.

The usual morning sounds carried differently—Deanna's heels clicking down the hallway, the electric kettle sputtering its warning, Isla's soft footsteps as she padded into the kitchen with her hair tangled and her eyes still full of sleep. Everything unfolded the same as always, and yet…

Yet, something had changed.

Aurora could feel it the moment she stepped onto the landing.

She wasn't holding her breath.

Not fully.

There had always been a ritual to the way she moved through the house. A choreography of survival. Step softly past the bathroom. Don't make eye contact in the kitchen. Speak only when spoken to, and even then, with caution. Brace for impact. Always.

But today, her body moved differently.

Looser. Slower.

She descended the stairs like someone testing the floorboards.

When she walked into the kitchen, Deanna glanced at her briefly, then turned back to her toast.

That was all.

No snarl. No performance. No icy commentary on her face or her outfit or the way her hair looked "like a brushfire."

It wasn't love. But it was the absence of cruelty.

And that felt damn good.

Graham was already sitting at the table with his perpetual mug of coffee and the morning paper folded in half beside him. The radio was playing quietly. The volume low, like a secret.

He looked up when she entered.

"Morning, kiddo."

Aurora blinked. She looked behind herself to see if Vanessa had arrived in the kitchen at the same time as her.

It wasn't the words—it was the tone. The warmth. Not exaggerated. Not pitying. Just... normal. Like she was someone who lived here. Someone who belonged.

She moved toward the cupboard and headed back to the table with her bowl.

He reached across the table and slid the box of cereal toward her without a word.

And she stayed.

That evening, she stayed. The next evening, she stayed. And every evening after that, she stayed.

Not because everything was fixed. Not because she felt safe. But because this time—finally—someone had stood up for her. For once, she hadn't been cast out.

And that was enough to keep her in the house.

That night—just another night in this alternate timeline, not one of high hopes or dreams fulfilled, but one marked by the *bare minimums* a child should be able to expect—she lay on her bed with the lights off. A blanket pulled to her chin. Her headphones resting around her neck.

She stared at the ceiling and let the stillness settle over her like a weighted sheet.

Around eight o'clock, there was a knock.

Not sharp. Not impatient.

Just... there.

She sat up.

"Yeah?" Her voice cracked. She hated that.

The door creaked open.

Graham stood in the hallway, one hand on the knob, the other in the pocket of his sweater. The light behind him framed him in soft gold. He looked older than usual. Not tired. Just real.

"I made tea," he said.

She didn't answer.

"I put cinnamon in it," he added. "I thought you might like that."

She did. She'd never told him that.

She nodded once.

He didn't press her. Just stepped inside and handed her the mug. It was warm in her hands, heavy and earthy and perfectly full.

She took a sip.

It tasted like memory. Like something she hadn't let herself want.

He sat at the edge of her desk chair, facing her, but not too close.

They didn't talk.

For a long while, they just existed in the same space. The tea cooled between them. Her breathing evened out.

Finally, she whispered, "Why now?"

He looked at her.

"What do you mean?"

She shrugged, eyes fixed on the mug in her lap. "Why'd you say something? The other day. You never—" She stopped. Started again. "You've never done that before."

Graham was quiet for a moment.

Then he said, simply, "Because I saw your face."

Aurora glanced up, startled.

"I've seen you angry before. Annoyed. Snarky." He gave a small, tired smile. "That one's kind of your default."

She almost smiled back.

"But I've never seen you look scared like that," he continued. "And I realized… I've been watching it happen for years. Pretending it wasn't as bad as it was. Telling myself she's just stressed. Or you're just dramatic."

She winced.

"But that wasn't it," he said. "You looked scared. And I didn't want to be the kind of man who let that happen in his house."

The words hovered.

They didn't fix anything. Not immediately.

But they built something.

A first brick.

A first nail.

A place to begin.

Aurora didn't cry.

But she sipped the rest of her tea.

And didn't ask him to leave.

Over the next few months, her body began to unlearn its defenses.

The way she used to flinch when Deanna entered the room—gone.

The way she used to sleep with her door locked—no longer necessary.

The way her voice used to shrink mid-sentence, waiting for someone to cut her off—steadier now.

It wasn't that Deanna changed. Not really. But she'd been interrupted. And the edge of her cruelty dulled when no one sharpened it for her.

Aurora still had bad days.

Still snapped. Still sulked. Still skipped class once in a while, still smoked behind the school and pretended she didn't care about anything.

But she stayed.

When she could have left.

She stayed.

She stayed for Isla, who left notes on her pillow that said *I missed you today,* and *can you braid my hair tomorrow?*

She stayed for Graham, who made pancakes every Sunday now—too thick, too dense, but made with both hands and a sense of purpose.

She stayed for herself.

Because her room was finally hers again.

Because her music sounded louder without the fear.

Because the house hadn't become a home, not yet.

But it wasn't the war zone it used to be.

And sometimes, when she walked through the door after school, her father looked up from the couch and said, *Welcome back,* like her presence here mattered.

Like *she* mattered.

And in the deepest part of her, something that had once curled up and gone quiet began to stretch.

To breathe.

To believe.

*****

It was a Tuesday. Or maybe a Thursday. The kind of day you forget, unless it becomes the reason everything changed.

The hallway was dim, washed in the watery afternoon light that filtered through the high window at the end of the corridor. It made everything look dustier, older—like the house itself had paused to listen.

Isla was ten. Too quiet. Too small for her age. She wore a sweater two sizes too big and held a pen in her hand like it was something precious. Vanessa had just turned Twelve and was standing over her like a queen surveying something unworthy.

Aurora had left the house an hour ago. Deanna was in the den with a glass of wine and a stack of catalogues she would never order from. Graham was supposed to be working late.

But he wasn't.

He was standing at the top of the stairs, just out of sight, watching.

Vanessa's voice was soft. Deceptively so. "I told you not to take my pen."

"I didn't mean to," Isla whispered. "I just—I needed one. I didn't know it was yours." The pen in question was nothing special—black ink, plastic barrel, *Bic* embossed faintly along the side.

"You don't need anything of mine," Vanessa said, her face too close now. "You just take. Because you're weak. Because you know no one will stop you."

Isla shrank back, the pen falling from her fingers.

Vanessa leaned in, her mouth near her sister's ear. "You're nothing without other people. A leech. You always have been."

She wasn't yelling. That was the worst part.

She didn't need to.

Graham cleared his throat.

The sound was small. A cough, maybe. A shift of presence.

But Vanessa stilled like she'd been slapped.

She turned slowly, her expression flickering through surprise, embarrassment, and finally—something else. Something young.

He didn't shout.

Didn't demand an explanation.

Just stepped into the hallway, his voice quiet, even.

"Isla," he said. "Go see if your mom needs anything, okay?"

Isla nodded quickly. She didn't run. But she wanted to.

The moment the soft thud of her socks faded, Graham turned to his middle daughter.

She was standing straight. Chin up. Arms folded across her chest like armor.

She waited for his anger.

It didn't come.

"I heard what you said," he told her.

She looked away. "It was just a joke."

"No, it wasn't."

She swallowed.

"I don't know what's going on," he said. "At school, in your head, with Mom. I don't know what made you feel like you needed to say that to your sister. I don't know what makes you feel like you should treat her that way."

Vanessa blinked. Her eyes were glassy now. But she didn't let the tears fall.

"But that," he continued, "isn't okay. And I'm not going to let it become who you are."

Her face crumpled for the smallest second. She covered it fast.

"Do you want to be like Mom?" he asked gently.

"No."

"Then you have to stop this now."

She looked at him. Really looked.

And for the first time in a long time, she saw him. Not the absent, watchful man she'd learned to so easily manipulate—but someone present. Someone awake.

And it scared her.

But it also—maybe—saved her.

That was the last time she spoke to Isla that way.

Not because she got caught.

But because she got seen.

It didn't happen overnight.

But something shifted inside Vanessa after that.

She stopped talking about Isla like a weight. Started talking about her like a puzzle—still strange, but interesting. She rolled her eyes at her, yes. Still criticized her choice of socks and the books she read. But she didn't touch her.

Didn't corner her.

Didn't *bruise* her. Not with hands. Not with words.

When she saw Isla curled up in the corner of the couch crying over a math grade, she brought her a cookie and walked away before Isla could ask why.

In the real timeline, Vanessa never softened.

But here?

In this version?

She doesn't become a villain.

She doesn't inherit Deanna's poison unfiltered.

She's still sharp. Still ambitious. Still quick to dominate a conversation.

But she uses it differently.

In university, she studies psychology instead of pre-law for her undergrad before continuing on to law school. Not because it's easy, but because it's necessary. Because she wants to understand why people hurt each other. Why *she* almost did.

She writes essays about emotional intelligence and power dynamics. Submits research papers on generational trauma. Volunteers at a crisis hotline.

When a freshman roommate has a panic attack in the middle of the night, it's Vanessa who stays with her. Who knows what to say.

Because someone once told her:
You're not a monster.
But you could become one.
And I won't let that happen.

Years later, Isla will say, in a speech at Vanessa's graduation: "I wouldn't be here if not for my sister."

And Vanessa, eyes full, won't deny it.

She'll just reach for Isla's hand.

And squeeze.

*****

It started with space.

Not physical space—there was never much of that in the house on Ashbury Lane—but emotional space. The room to exhale. To exist without apology. To feel without flinching.

Isla Lockwood grew up in that space..

No one remembered the shift exactly. Just that one day, no one raised their voice when a glass was dropped in the kitchen. That the air didn't tense when Isla walked into a room. That her own name, once so often spoken like a sigh, began to sound like something cherished.

"Aurora," Graham would say from the doorway, soft as dusk. "Want to help me with the garden?"

Or from across the table at dinner: "Isla, what did you write today?"

He asked like all three of his daughters' thoughts mattered. Like they were all worth making time for.

And Deanna—while still complicated, still brittle in many ways—was quieter now. More watchful. Her sharp edges no longer encouraged. Her cruelty no longer unchecked. And so, she stayed quieter. Bit her tongue. Left rooms instead of tearing them apart.

That alone rewrote the Lockwoods' entire world.

For Isla, she began to speak.

Not just with words, but with posture. She stopped curling into herself, stopped clutching her elbows like she was trying to vanish into her own ribs.

She sang sometimes.

Not loudly. But when she thought no one was listening, she hummed little tunes under her breath—melodies from childhood movies, songs she made up on the spot, scraps of poems she'd written the night before and hadn't yet put to paper.

Aurora heard her once.

Didn't say a word.

Just left a notebook on Isla's pillow that night with a post-it note that said: *Use this. You're magic.*

Isla cried when she read it.

Then filled almost half of the pages by morning.

She became a creature of softness, not of fear.

She liked rainy days best—curled up in the big chair by the window, her feet tucked under her, a library book in his girls' lap and a cup of tea that Graham had made just how she liked it. Too much honey, not enough steeping time. She never corrected him.

She kept paper cranes taped to her mirror. Tended to a tiny jade plant she'd named Clementine. Wrote stories about girls who talked to birds and boys who turned into trees.

Her bedroom was yellow. She'd picked the colour herself—a pale, buttery gold that turned warm in the sunlight. The paint was uneven in some places where her hand had wobbled, but she didn't mind. It felt like hers.

Her world expanded slowly.

She made friends at school. The kind who asked her real questions and waited for the answers. The kind who didn't laugh when she stammered. She joined the library club. Got asked to help design the school's poetry zine and to perform her work out loud. Started wearing mismatched socks on purpose, just because she liked the look of lavender next to seafoam green.

Graham drove her to every reading.

Even the ones no one else came to.

He'd sit in the back row, hands folded, smiling like she was the only voice in the world.

At thirteen, she told him she was afraid of getting older.

"Why?" he asked.

"Because what if I stop being soft?" she said. "What if the world turns me into someone who yells all the time? Like Mom used to?"

He knelt beside her. Touched her cheek like something sacred.

"You won't," he said. "You were born with gentleness. That's not weakness, Isla. That's your gift."

She remembered that sentence forever.

She wrote it in the front of every journal she ever kept.

At fourteen, she had her first panic attack.

It came out of nowhere—at least, it felt that way. In the middle of a class presentation. Her throat closed up. Her hands went numb. Her vision pinched at the edges.

She ran.

The school called Graham.

He came in ten minutes.

Found her sitting on the curb out front, knees pulled to her chest, hands shaking.

He didn't ask what happened.

He just sat down beside her and passed her a bottle of water.

"You're okay," he said. "We'll figure this out."

And they did.

Therapy. Breathing tools. A quiet understanding that she didn't have to be perfect to be loved.

When they got home that night, Aurora had already filled the tub with warm water and candles. Vanessa left her a lavender sleep mask on the pillow.

No one said anything.

But Isla felt it.

She was held.

She grew up like ivy on a sun-warmed wall.

Still quiet. Still thoughtful.

But never again afraid to speak.

She read. She wrote. She painted little watercolour moons on the backs of receipts and left them in Graham's jacket pockets like little spells. She saved movie tickets. Kept birthday cards. Learned to bake.

At seventeen, she submitted a poem to a local lit journal.

It was accepted.

She brought the magazine home and placed it on Graham's desk without a word.

He read it three times.

Cried.

Framed the page.

She didn't even mind.

In this version of her life, no one took her softness and turned it into something to mock.

No one stepped on her voice before it had the chance to rise.

In this version of her life, Isla Lockwood didn't survive childhood.

She *grew up* in it.

And that changed everything.

*****

Aurora grew up, too—but not in exile.

Not in panic. Not in defiance. Not by surviving what should have broken her.

She grew up in a house that made room for her. One that no longer echoed with accusation. One where she was no longer the problem, the scapegoat, the storm.

In this version of her life, she wasn't walking on eggshells. She wasn't trying to be invisible, or unbothered, or less.

She got to be loud, sometimes. She got to be wrong.

And no one used it against her.

She still kept her headphones on more than she needed to. Still rolled her eyes at the world. Still pulled her sleeves down past her knuckles. But now, when she slammed a door, someone knocked. Not to punish her. Just to ask if she was okay.

It was Graham, usually.

He didn't always know what to say.

But he came.

Once, after a fight with Deanna about her curfew, Aurora locked herself in her room for five hours. She expected to find cold dinner when she finally emerged. Instead, she found a plate still warm in the oven. A note folded in Graham's handwriting: *You're allowed to be mad. But I still want you to eat.*

She didn't say anything. Just sat on the kitchen stool and ate slowly, while Graham cleaned dinner dishes like nothing had happened.

When Aurora started writing music, it wasn't in secret.

She wrote at the kitchen table.

In the living room.

Once, on the porch with Isla reading beside her, her foot tapping in quiet rhythm.

She filled notebook after notebook with lyrics and chords and fragments of something too big to hold in her chest. Sometimes she sang softly to herself while she scribbled. Sometimes louder. No one told her to stop.

One afternoon, Graham leaned against the doorframe and said, "That new one—you play it like you mean it."

Aurora didn't look up. But her pencil paused. "Do I?"

He nodded. "Yeah. Like it's yours."

It was the closest thing to praise she'd ever expected. It landed in her ribs like a light being turned on.

She shared things more slowly than Isla did. But when she shared them, she meant it.

She started letting Isla read her lyrics. Let Vanessa borrow her CDs. When Isla asked if she could learn guitar, Aurora didn't say no. She just handed over her oldest pick and said, "Try not to break it."

She wasn't easy.

But she didn't have to be.

She still left eventually.

Of course she did.

That was always in her—flight. Curiosity. Distance.

But when she did, it wasn't a running. It wasn't an escape.

She left with a suitcase full of songs, a rented apartment with a leaky window, and a list of names she could call if everything went wrong.

Graham drove her to the bus station. Carried her amp like it wasn't too heavy. He didn't say much on the ride. Just handed her a to-go coffee with *extra sugar* and asked if she remembered to pack a jacket.

When she boarded, he stood on the platform with his hands in his pockets, watching her go.

He waved.

That was all.

But she saw it.

And that was everything.

She called home.

Not because she had to.

But because she wanted to.

Sometimes just to talk. Sometimes just to hear her sisters' voices. She sent postcards. Wrote notes on the back of gig flyers. Left voicemails that started with "You won't believe what happened tonight."

And every time she came back?

There was a plate at the table.

A clean towel on her bed.

A home that hadn't thrown her out.

Because in this version of her life, Aurora Lockwood didn't have to burn down to be free.

She just had to be loved.

And she was.

*****

The house itself changed.

It felt bigger, even though it wasn't. The walls stretched with laughter. The windows let in more light. The cold parts—the hallway, the north-facing bathroom, the back stairwell—seemed to soften.

They started leaving the door open in the evenings.

Not always locked. Not always guarded.

Neighbours stopped by. Friends from school. Partners and crushes and quiet kids with soft voices and purple hair who Isla called "my people." They stayed for dinner. Sat on the floor with mugs of tea. Brought records and borrowed books and helped repaint the downstairs bathroom one summer just because they wanted to.

Aurora strung fairy lights along the banister. Vanessa brought home throw pillows that didn't match. Graham didn't complain. He bought a lavender candle one day just because Isla said she liked it.

The house smelled like baking and fabric softener and incense and pine.

It smelled like home.

There was a night in late spring when it all came together. Nothing special marked it—not a birthday, not a holiday. Just a warm breeze through the open windows and the soft haze of early dusk settling over the roof.

Aurora was home for the weekend. Vanessa had brought a record from a street market in Montreal. Isla had made lemon bars that mostly held their shape.

Graham put on the record.

It crackled.

Then swelled into something soft and old and unbearably sweet.

Deanna, who spent so much of her time on the outskirts, watching with dark eyes, stood, laced her fingers between Graham's. They danced.

In the kitchen. In the living room. On the back porch beneath the windchimes.

The girls joined in.

Vanessa twirled Isla until they both fell down laughing.

Graham kissed Deanna on the cheek and took Aurora's hands and spun her around, badly, like he hadn't danced in twenty years.

And for a moment—just one golden, glowing moment—the house itself seemed to exhale.

As if it, too, had been waiting for this life to arrive.

As if it, too, had dreamed of being filled not with silence or fear, but with music.

And warmth.

And love.

*****

Vanessa Lockwood didn't grow up soft.

But she didn't need to grow up hard.

Because in this life—the one where Graham spoke up, and kept speaking—she didn't have to build her power out of cruelty.

She still had fire. Still held herself like a woman who would never be overlooked. She was quick, razor-sharp, always two moves ahead. But she no longer used those gifts to manipulate or wound. Because they weren't the only tools she was given.

Graham made sure of it.

He didn't shame her for being forceful. He didn't tell her to quiet down, to be easier, sweeter, smaller. He told her to *aim it*.

To sharpen her insight. To take that spine of steel and wrap it in purpose.

She listened.

Eventually.

It didn't happen all at once. It took years—of redirection, of consequence, of love that held its ground. But somewhere between majoring in psychology and winning her first case in court, she became someone who used her fire to protect, not destroy.

She became a lawyer. Not because she wanted money, though the money came—but because she had things to say, and now she knew how to say them.

She fought for women who had no one else. Took on corporations. Stared down boardrooms full of men with padded resumes and slippery morals and never blinked. She wrote her own rules. Enforced them with elegance.

She married someone who wasn't afraid of her.

His name was Thomas. He wore beautifully tailored suits and made terrible pancakes, just like Graham, and loved their children with a steadiness that made Vanessa fall for him all over again, every Sunday.

They had two daughters—Nora and Elise. Both loud. Both brilliant. Both wildly different.

Vanessa didn't try to shape them.

She guided them.

She caught their worst days without judgment. Apologized when she got it wrong. Made them scrambled eggs and coffee and stood in the doorway of their bedrooms just to watch them exist.

Graham visited every few months. Sometimes just for a day. Sometimes longer.

He brought lemon drops for the girls, even though they didn't like them. He always forgot.

But they loved that he brought them anyway.

They called him Pop.

He let them paint his nails blue once.

Vanessa took a picture.

Framed it.

Set it on her desk at work.

*****

The family wasn't perfect.

Not every dinner was calm. Not every holiday was free from tension. Sometimes old wounds ached in new weather. Sometimes Graham and Deanna passed each other like shadows at events—civil, distant, complicated in the way long marriages sometimes are.

But the house was never cruel again.

That mattered.

There was room now—for laughter and mistakes, for quiet and correction, for music and mess and growth.

It wasn't perfect.

But it was safe.

And that changed everything.

*****

It started years later with a roast chicken.

Not because Graham was good at cooking—he wasn't, not at first—but because it felt like something that could hold them together as the girls grew into adults. A centrepiece. A ritual. A kind of scaffolding around which the rest of their lives might take shape.

He started small. A recipe printed off the internet, slightly crumpled and flattened on the counter with a spoon. Salt and pepper. Carrots cut too thick. Potatoes that stayed hard in the middle, but smelled good enough to mask the flaw. He opened all the windows and let the house fill with rosemary and lemon and the sizzle of heat on metal—then texted all three daughters in the group chat all five Lockwoods somehow kept alive, thick with memes and check-ins and the occasional photo of a dog in a sweater.

Aurora was the first arrive on that inaugural Sunday.

She didn't say anything. Just walked into the kitchen, lifted the lid on the roasting pan, and tried not to make a face.

"Bold choice," she muttered. She and Deanna laughed about it together.

But Aurora didn't leave.

Isla arrived second and set the table.

Vanessa appeared ten minutes late with a sarcastic compliment about the "ambience," but she brought ice cream for dessert, and that felt like peace.

They all sat.

And they ate.

It became a tradition—not by decree, but by repetition.

Every Sunday, without fail, Graham made dinner.

He got better at it. Learned how to blanch green beans and keep them crisp. Learned to pull the chicken out just before the juices ran clear. Learned that Isla hated thyme, that Vanessa liked things arranged by colour, that Aurora would always pretend she wasn't hungry and then steal food off other people's plates after her meager serving was consumed.

They teased each other. Even Deanna could be the butt of a subtle jab.

They passed rolls.

Argued about movies and song lyrics and what counted as "classic" literature.

Sometimes they laughed so hard that Graham had to set his fork down and hold his ribs. Sometimes Deanna snorted when she laughed. Aurora once spilled a full glass of water and Vanessa made a scene out of it so theatrical, Isla wrote a poem about it called Floodplain.

The space and the time had been claimed.

And it was theirs.

Music became part of it.

Aurora made playlists—sometimes themed, sometimes chaotic. One week it was 70s soul. The next, punk. Once, she played an entire dinner's worth of songs that included the word *moon* in the title.

Vanessa pretended to be annoyed.

But she hummed along to every tune.

Isla brought candles to the table. Different ones each week. Cinnamon apple. Sandalwood. Fresh linen. Graham never remembered to blow them out, so the kitchen always smelled faintly of something sweet the next morning.

They added things, little by little.

Cloth napkins from a thrift store Deanna loved.

A string of fairy lights around the windows.

Aurora started making dessert—badly, but with enthusiasm. Her apple crumble was closer to soup. Her brownies came out like bricks. Everyone ate them anyway.

Vanessa brought sparkling water and fancy juice and once, a bottle of cheap prosecco she claimed was "just for the aesthetic."

Graham raised a glass and toasted to the aesthetic.

One night, they all stayed at the table long after the plates were empty.

The candles burned low. The playlist had looped back to the beginning. Outside, the wind was knocking softly against the windows, and the sky had gone the kind of purple that only happens in spring—deep and bruised, but soft around the edges.

Aurora was talking about a music venue in Philadelphia. Isla was curled into her chair, legs tucked up under her, smiling. Vanessa was peeling the label off another bottle of Prosecco, humming along to a song that had once made her cry.

Graham looked at them.

All three of them.

His girls.

And for the first time in his life, he didn't feel like he was waiting for something to go wrong.

He felt here.

In the warmth. In the noise. In the little clinks of forks and glasses and Isla's quiet giggle when Vanessa swatted Aurora's hand away from her plate.

This was the life they had built together.

Not a palace.

But a table.

Set with intention.

Lit by grace.

Held up by second chances.

Years later, when Isla tried to write about it—when she wanted to capture what those nights had meant—she couldn't.

Not fully.

She wrote, instead:
The chicken was never perfect.
The music was too loud.
Vanessa drank too much soda and Aurora used her fork like a drumstick.
But I've never felt safer than at that table.
I've never laughed louder.
I've never been more known.

Graham framed it.

Hung it in the hallway.

Right next to the light switch.

So he'd see it every time he left a room.

And remember what they made together.

Every Sunday.

Every ordinary, sacred Sunday.

*****

Graham Lockwood died on a Wednesday.

It was raining—steady, soft, the kind of rain that stayed for hours, soaking into the soil like something holy.

He was seventy-nine.

He passed in his favourite chair, by the window in Aurora's old bedroom, now a reading room filled with plants and sunlight. A half-finished crossword lay on the table beside him. A blanket knitted by Isla draped across his lap.

All three daughters were there. Deanna had passed just months before him.

Aurora had flown in from Seattle. Her hair was even longer now, streaked with white that gave a feeling of highlights rather than age, tied back in a scarf patterned with tiny suns. She held his hand through the morning and sang to him when he started to slip.

Isla curled beside his chair on the floor, reading softly from his favourite book of poetry. Her voice cracked on the last stanza, but she kept going.

Vanessa stood at the window, arms crossed, silent and still. Watching the rain. The trees. The way the world kept moving even when your heart wanted it to stop.

When it was time, they gathered around him.

They didn't beg him to stay.

They just stayed with him.

And when his breath slowed and softened and finally stopped, the room stayed warm.

Full.

Whole.

*****

They buried him beneath the plum tree in the backyard. The one Isla used to cry beneath in some other timeline, in some other version of their lives. The one Isla had decorated with paper lanterns the year she turned eighteen. The one Graham used to lean against while watching his girls laugh under the stars.

Isla wrote the eulogy. Vanessa read it. Aurora sang afterward, her voice low and unadorned, the way Graham had always liked best.

They held each other.

Not as survivors.

But as daughters of a man who had learned to stay.

The Awakening ~ Graham Present Day

It slipped away slowly.

Like mist dissolving in morning light. Like a dream he wasn't ready to leave.

One moment, he was there—sitting at a long kitchen table bathed in warm afternoon sun, music floating from somewhere just out of sight. Isla's soft laugh. Aurora's voice rising in a story that had everyone's eyes shining. Vanessa, arguing an opinion respectfully. Deanna, her hand resting lightly on his, a glass of sparkling water catching the light between them. A cake in the centre of the table. A candle lit. One of the girls—he couldn't remember which—was singing.

It was perfect.

No. It was true. In the dream, it felt more real than anything had in years.

But then came the light.

Real light.

Paler. Less golden. Cutting in through the crooked blinds like an uninvited guest. The hum of the fridge. The faint ache in his knees. The smell of dust and stale coffee.

The kitchen was empty.

The house was quiet.

Not warm.

Just still.

Graham blinked against it, breath caught in his throat. He wasn't at the sun-drenched table. There was no music. No candles. No laughter.

Just him.

Alone.

At the scarred, unadorned kitchen table, where one of the chairs still wobbled, and the linoleum beneath his slippers curled up at the edges.

Deanna was dead—and in this timeline, that somehow felt like the easing of a burden rather than a heart-piercing sorrow.

He sat back, heart thudding—not in panic, but in loss.

Because for one fleeting, brilliant moment, he had seen it. Felt it.

The life they could have had.

It clung to his skin like the after image of light.

And for a moment—just a moment—he couldn't breathe.

He pressed a hand to his face, fingers trembling, and tried to steady himself.

But the truth was there now. The other timeline. The one with dinners and music and laughter that didn't hurt.

The one where Aurora hadn't left. Where Vanessa had grown into someone fierce but kind. Where Isla had blossomed early—instead of quietly fading into herself, only finding her voice after escaping the family she'd come to see as both swamp and noose around her neck.

He saw it. All of it. Every missed chance. Every word he didn't say. Every door he let close. Every time he blamed Deanna alone because he couldn't bear to look inward.

A sound escaped him. A dry, broken thing. He pressed his palm to his mouth, but it didn't stop the next one.

He cried.

Not loudly. Not messily.

But with the grief of an old man who had just glimpsed the life he threw away.

His shoulders shook once. Then again.

And then it passed.

He wiped his eyes on his sleeve. Sniffed.

Then, slowly—almost reflexively—he began to tuck it all back inside.

The gymnastics began the way they always did: subtly, then all at once.

He leaned back in his chair and let the weight of memory settle in a way that didn't hurt as much. He began to rearrange things. Just a little.

It had never really been his fault.

Deanna had been the one who yelled. Deanna had always had the temper, the sharp tongue, the wine in her hand at two in the afternoon. She had set the tone. She had shaped the walls. She had taught the girls how to fear, how to walk on eggshells. He... he was just trying to keep the peace.

That's what men were told to do, wasn't it?

Don't escalate. Don't make it worse. Stay calm. Stay quiet.

And hadn't he done that?

He hadn't screamed. He hadn't hit anyone. He went to work, paid the bills, kept the furnace running, showed up for parent-teacher conferences. When the girls cried, he'd offered tissues. He didn't start the fires—he just watched them burn. That wasn't the same as lighting the match.

And Aurora—God, Aurora. She had always been a firecracker. Impossible to please. Always mouthing off, pushing buttons. She would've left no matter what he did. And Vanessa—well, she'd always been difficult, too. Oppositional. Challenging. Deanna was harder on her than he liked, sure, but he'd always stepped in—not *just* to protect her, but to make sure she faced no consequence. Still, he told himself, he hadn't created Vanessa's edge. That had been there from the start.

And Isla?

Well, Isla was fine now.

She'd always been sensitive. She cried easily. Took things personally. He remembered her once sobbing for hours because a teacher raised their voice. He and Deanna had laughed about it at the time—so dramatic. But look at her now. She got married. She wrote books. Travelled. Had a life. Wasn't that proof that nothing had been ruined?

They all turned out fine, really.

Considering.

And he wasn't Deanna.

That was the most important thing.

She had been cruel. He hadn't.

She had lashed out. He hadn't.

She had failed them.

He had... endured it. Endured *them*. Kept his head down. Stayed quiet. Survived.

And for Graham, survival had always seemed like enough.

Hadn't it?

He told himself so. Again and again. That *not causing* harm was the same as preventing it. That staying neutral was a kind of virtue. That letting Deanna rage unchecked made him blameless by default.

But no matter how the story unfolded in his mind—no matter how much weight he placed on her cruelty, or their chaos, or his own weariness—Graham would never see it.

Would never name it.

Would never understand that the nothing he did for his daughters had always been the problem.

The light through the blinds shifted again. Dust floated in the air, catching gold along the edges. The silence in the house wasn't comforting. But it wasn't unbearable, either.

He stood. Poured himself another cup of coffee. Sat down again.

The dream was already beginning to blur. Already softening at the edges. The music, the laughter, the candlelight—all folding back into shadow. It had never really happened, after all.

It was just a fantasy.

A trick of the mind.

And he had a life to live.

No sense mourning a world that never existed.

Especially when he was never the one who broke it.

What's Left ~ Aurora Present Day

The letter came folded inside a manila envelope, creased neatly down the centre, sealed with the kind of distance Deanna always used to mistake for control. There was no handwriting on the front. Just Aurora's name, typed in tidy all caps. A file number in the corner. Clinical.

She'd been sitting in the lawyer's office when she received it. She'd been called in separately to her sisters. The air smelled like dust and lemon polish. No one else was there—no Vanessa, no Isla. Just Aurora, the lawyer, and a silence that felt weighted, like something had been waiting too long to be said.

"This is separate from the estate," the lawyer said. "She left instructions that this be given to you directly. And only to you."

Aurora didn't open it then.

She didn't need to.

She already knew it would feel too late.

She waited until she got home.

She poured herself a drink. Sat on the edge of her bathtub, fully clothed, the envelope balanced on her knees like something fragile and radioactive.

Then, she opened it.

My Aurora,

If you're reading this, I'm gone. And this is the first time I've ever really spoken to you without rage between us. I don't expect forgiveness. I wouldn't know what to do with it even if you gave it. But I need you to hear me.

We had a hard relationship. You were so much of who I wanted to be—and I think, deep down, I resented that. Because I was terrified of my own mother. My father. My first husband. Everyone, really. I could never be myself.

I ran away when I was fifteen.

I'd already dropped out before my first day of high school. I was pregnant. My older brother Bert took me in—he and his wife Daisy let me sleep in their basement. I never told you or your sisters about that child. A boy. I gave him up for adoption. His father was the kind of cruel that wears a wedding ring. When I tried to go back home, my father, Harry, told me I'd made my bed.

So I learned to lie in it.

I thought the best I'd ever get was someone willing to keep me. Someone who didn't hit. Someone who saw me and didn't walk away. When I met your father, Graham, I thought maybe that was him. I got pregnant by accident—on purpose. I was afraid he'd leave if I didn't give him a reason to stay. So we rushed. Got married. Built a life I didn't know how to live in.

For a while, it worked.

And then it didn't.

He laughed at my music. Not in the playful way. In the mean way. The superior way. He teased me about what I ate until I stopped eating in front of anyone at all. Then he mocked me as anorexic. He mocked everything I loved–quietly, passively–until I stopped loving it.

And then he went quiet.

Nothing I did could shake him out of it. Except Vanessa. She was the only one he seemed to care about. The two of them had a bond I could never touch. And slowly, I became a stranger in a life I'd built. Locked in. Trapped.

And I turned that hurt outward.

At you, first.

Then Isla.

Never Vanessa–Graham would step in if it was her. Not to stop me, but to protect her. And even for her, when she started to slip, when she needed a parent and not a pedestal, he had nothing left to give.

But, this isn't about her. This is about you.

I want you to know that I see it now.

All of it.

I hurt you.

I punished you for who I could never be. For everything I lost. I told myself you were strong enough to take it. But you were a child. And I should've been the one standing between you and the fire, not lighting it.

I regret what I did.

I regret who I became.

And I know that regret won't fix anything. I know it doesn't change what I took from you, and what I took from myself.

But still—I want you to know: I loved you.

Always.

Even when I couldn't show it.

Even when I twisted it into something else.

You were never hard to love, Aurora.

I just didn't know how to hold anything without crushing it.
Love,
Mom

Aurora read it once.

Then again.

The third time, her eyes didn't move. They just stared at the page, unmoving, unblinking. Her jaw was clenched so tightly her ears rang.

She folded the letter in half. Creased it along the same centre line Deanna had. Then again. Into quarters. Into eighths.

But she didn't tear it.

Not with rage.

Not even with grief.

She just held it.

Held it like a bruise. Like proof. Like something she'd carried for years and only now had the shape of.

She found Isla later that night. She was sitting on the front steps of their childhood home, arms wrapped around her knees, hair pulled into a loose bun at the nape of her neck. The porch light hummed overhead. The house behind them was dark.

"She left me a letter," Aurora said, sitting down beside her.

Isla turned her head. "Deanna?" She often did that—forgot to call her Mom. She was married now, closer to her mother-in-law than she'd ever been to the jagged edge of the woman who raised her.

Aurora nodded. "She told the truth," she said. "Finally. At the very end."

"What did she say?"

"That she was sorry. That she loved me. That she'd always loved me. And that she didn't know how to show it."

Isla didn't speak right away.

Then she said, "That must've been hard to read."

"It was," Aurora said. "But it helped, too." There was silence for a moment. It stretched between them like something new. Not heavy. Not broken. Just... real.

"She hurt us," Isla said. "Both of them did."

"I know."

"But I think I can miss her now," Isla added quietly. "Just a little."

Aurora looked up at the stars.

"I think I already do."

They sat like that for a long time in silence. Not the good kind of silence. But not the bad kind either.

The kind that makes room.

The kind that lets you breathe.

The kind that follows truth.

And makes space for whatever comes next.

Part III
The Reckoning

The Hearing ~ Three Sisters Present Day

The courtroom was cold.

Not physically—though the marble floors didn't help—but in the way rooms become when grief and resentment collide with exhaustion and exasperation. The air had a sharpness to it. Clean, expensive, surgical. Like nothing human could grow here. Just wounds.

Vanessa sat, flanked not by an attorney but by rage, self-righteous indignation, and emotional armour polished to perfection. Her black suit was immaculate—tailored within an inch of its life—and her hair twisted into an elegant chignon. Her expression was neutral. Composed. But her eyes burned. She had been preparing for this moment for weeks.

The will was wrong.

She would prove it, or so she claimed.

On the other side of the room, Aurora and Isla sat shoulder to shoulder—an unlikely unity, but a necessary one, and one both sisters found themselves grateful for. Aurora in grey. Isla in green. Neither of them spoke as Vanessa's voice filled the courtroom like steel drawn from a sheath.

"My mother was not a sentimental woman," Vanessa began, her voice clipped and precise. "But she was intentional. She didn't leave behind a long paper trail. She didn't write birthday cards. But she said what she meant, and she meant what she said."

She paused, letting the silence settle.

"I was with her when she said the ring would be mine. My grandmother's engagement ring—eighteen karat white gold, solitaire diamond. It belonged to my father's mother, and it was promised to me. Not once. Many times."

Vanessa nodded to herself, flipping slowly through the file. "What's outlined in this will contradicts her stated intentions," Vanessa continued. "She may not have put it in writing, but she was clear. This ring was never meant for Isla."

Her gaze didn't flick toward her sisters. It landed.

"It was a mistake," she said calmly. "And mistakes should be corrected, even if my sister's don't want them to be."
Then she sat down.

The room exhaled, felt lighter somehow without Vanessa's steam and venom in it.

It wasn't long before Isla was called to testify.

She rose slowly, hands clasped in front of her, and made her way to the stand. Her dress was simple, green, sleeves long. Her shoes creaked softly on the marble floor. She raised her right hand. Took the oath. Sat.

The judge asked her name. Her relationship to the deceased.

"I'm her youngest daughter," Isla replied.

There was a long pause before the next question came. "Would you consider your relationship with your mother to have been close?"

Another pause.

Then: "No."

Isla's response echoed.

"My mother and I didn't have a close relationship," Isla said calmly. "She didn't leave me much. That wasn't surprising. But she *did* leave me that ring. She left it because she wanted me to have something from Graham's side of the family. Something not tied to her. Something that might carry less pain."

She folded her hands in her lap.

She didn't raise her voice.

She didn't need to.

She stepped down. Her hands were trembling when she returned to her seat. Aurora reached over and took one. Isla didn't let go.

Then Aurora's name was called.

She stood slowly, the legs of her chair scraping against the floor. She was dressed in black, but not for mourning. She hadn't cried at the funeral. Not even once.

She walked to the stand.

She didn't hesitate.

The judge went through the formalities and then asked if she had a statement.

She nodded.

Then spoke.

"Our mother wasn't kind," Aurora said evenly. "She wasn't generous. She wasn't nurturing. If she promised Vanessa the ring, she broke that promise. But Deanna Lockwood broke a *lot* of promises. That wasn't unique."

She didn't look at Vanessa. Just at the judge.

"She left that ring to Isla because she wanted to. Because she had time to reflect. Because at the end of everything—after all the bitterness and silence—she knew which of her daughters had been treated like an afterthought their whole life."

Aurora paused.

"Vanessa wasn't denied. She was challenged. And she doesn't know the difference."

Aurora's voice was cold. Clean. The kind of tone you use when you've already made peace with the fact that you won't be understood.

"She had our father's attention. All of it. Mom was an afterthought to Vanessa, someone she couldn't control anymore, so she turned to legacy. To objects. To symbols. She wants this ring not because she has emotional ties to it—but because she can't stand being told no."

A few feet away, Vanessa shifted in her seat.

Aurora didn't flinch.

"This ring isn't about inheritance," she said. "It's about ego. And I will not let her use mom's death to settle old scores."

She stepped down.

And the room stayed very, very still.

*****

The judge left to deliberate.

Fifteen minutes passed in silence.

Vanessa sat rigid, her fingers flexing against the curve of her armrest. Aurora stared straight ahead. Isla rubbed the edge of her sleeve between her thumb and forefinger.

The courtroom smelled like old wood and dried flowers. Like nothing living had been in it for years.

When the judge returned, the air shifted.

"The will stands," she said. "There is no evidence of verbal amendment or coercion. The item in question will remain in the possession of the named beneficiary."

There was a silence that rang like thunder.

Then Vanessa stood.

She didn't yell.

Didn't scream.

But the fury in her was volcanic.

She turned, slowly, her gaze landing on Isla with spite and venom. Then Aurora.

"This isn't over," she hissed.

Aurora raised an eyebrow. "Yes, it is," she bravely asserted.

Vanessa's jaw twitched.

But she said nothing else.

She turned on her heel and walked out, her heels echoing through the empty hallway like the last gasp of something ancient and bitter.

*****

Outside the courthouse, the air was warmer.

Isla stood with her coat clutched around her, looking up at the sky.

Aurora lit a cigarette. She didn't smoke anymore. But today, she let herself.

"You okay?" she asked quietly.

Isla nodded. "I think so."

There was a long pause.

Then Isla said, "She really believed she'd win. She really believed a simple ring was worth all of this."

"She's spent her whole life rewriting history," Aurora said as she exhaled smoke into the air. "She learned that from him," she added.

Then, softly, "But we didn't."

Isla smiled faintly. "No. We didn't."

They didn't speak after that.

They didn't need to.

Because some victories are quietly etched with deep fractures and breaks that make it all seem empty.

The Ashes And After ~ Aurora And Isla Present Day

The lake was cold that morning, blanketed in mist and silence. It didn't greet them. It didn't mourn. It simply existed—the way some places do, long after the memories formed there have soured into something quiet and sharp. Aurora stood with the urn in her gloved hands, her breath a ghost in the air. Isla beside her, small in her coat, clutching the zipper like it might hold her together. Neither of them spoke.

They had driven in silence. Three hours north of Jim Thorpe, away from the small town and grocery stores and old brick houses that still whispered of their childhood. The highway narrowed. The trees thickened. Eventually, the lake had emerged like a bruise between pines—silent, steel-grey, and endless. They parked at the same turnout as that day.

That day.

The one where Isla cried quietly in the backseat, after Deanna had humiliated her for something so small neither of them remembered what it was. Where Graham got out of the car to "get some air," and stood by the shore like he didn't hear it. Didn't hear her. Didn't see the pain written in the curve of her spine, the way she curled into herself.

"He didn't even look up," Isla said, voice flat now. She didn't mean it for discussion. Just to say it aloud. To give shape to the thing between them.

Aurora nodded. "No. He didn't."

The wind pushed across the lake, gentle but persistent. The kind of wind that found its way into every fold of your clothes, settled in your bones.

Aurora stepped closer to the water's edge. The ground was frozen beneath the layer of pine needles. The lake was still. Not a ripple.

There had been no funeral. No service. No slideshow of smiling photos, no softly played hymns. Graham had taken care of the legalities. But the rest—what to do with what was left—had fallen to Aurora and Isla. As if the final weight of their mother belonged only to the daughters she had harmed the most.

"Do you want to say anything?" Aurora asked.

Isla shook her head. "No. We said enough for a lifetime."

Aurora ran her thumb over the lid of the urn. It wasn't heavy. She'd expected it to be heavier. Somehow that felt unfair. All that hurt and vitriol—so small now. So portable.

They didn't dig.

They didn't pray.

Aurora opened the lid, and the first gust took some of their mother before she could even begin to spread the ashes.

She tilted the urn slowly, carefully. The ashes poured out in uneven clouds, the wind catching them and carrying them like dust, like secrets, like all the things he never said. Some of it landed on the surface of the lake, formed little constellations before dissolving into the dark water.

Isla stood perfectly still, her hands in her pockets. Her eyes were red, but she didn't cry. Not here.

When the last of the ashes were gone, Aurora closed the lid and set the empty container down on the frozen ground. She didn't bury it. She didn't throw it. She just let it be.

"I thought it would feel different," Isla said.

"How?"

"I don't know. She's really gone now, and I thought maybe that would mean something," Isla said thoughtfully.

Aurora looked at the lake. "It doesn't."

They stayed a while longer. Not for closure. There would never be closure. Just the echo of what should've been. The knowing. The remembering.

After a while, Aurora picked up the urn again. They turned away from the water.

They didn't say goodbye.

The Silence He Left Behind ~ Aurora And Isla Present Day

Graham Lockwood died in his chair on a Wednesday.

There was no warning. No build-up. No grand moment. Just a quiet stillness that slipped into the room and stayed.

The kettle had boiled dry. The TV remote lay on the armrest beside him. A crossword sat unfinished on the side table, a pencil resting neatly in its groove. Outside, rain tapped against the window in soft, uncertain rhythm.

No one was with him.

No one noticed he was gone until the neighbour realized the garbage bins hadn't been brought in. Until the mail began to stack up in the slot. Until the silence stopped being passive and became suspicious.

Vanessa hadn't spoken to him in months.

Still furious about the ring, still furious about the will, still furious that the world hadn't bent to her will the way she believed it should. She'd taken it out on Graham the way she took everything out on everyone—sharply, precisely, and without apology. Their last conversation had ended with the slam of a door and silence that stretched too long to take back.

By the time anyone found him, his body had settled.

The medical report said peaceful.

No one could confirm it.

Vanessa wept on social media.

She posted photos of him smiling faintly beside a potted fern, captions layered with heartbreak and hashtags. #RestEasyDad trailed beneath images of old birthday dinners, blurry selfies from better days that had never really existed.

In the videos, her voice cracked.

She told her followers about the devastation. About how cruel her sisters had been—how they'd taken the ring. How they'd refused to help. How they were leaving her to manage everything on her own.

She made it sound noble.

As if she had inherited *burden*, not just paperwork.

The truth was harder to photograph:
The house was his. Now hers.
But with it came debt, taxes, documents she didn't understand. There were unpaid bills tucked in drawers. Property assessments. Legal fees. The walls themselves felt heavy with it—responsibility she'd never learned to carry.

No one came to help.

Certainly not Aurora.

And definitely not Isla.

They didn't go to the house.

They didn't go to the funeral.

They didn't post.

They had dinner together the night the call came in. Quietly, plainly. No drama. No tears. Just a shared look when the voicemail finished playing. And then Aurora poured the wine.

They talked about their week. Isla's work. Aurora's latest song. A new recipe Isla had tried and nearly burned. Their husbands always running late for everything.

They talked about Graham eventually.

Not out of obligation.

But because there was space now—to talk honestly. Safely.

"He just… never showed up," Isla said, setting down her glass.

Aurora nodded. "That was his legacy. Not violence. Not cruelty. Just… silence."

They didn't speak with venom. There was no rage left. Only the dull ache of knowing how different it could have been.

"Vanessa's still trying to hurt us," Isla said quietly.

"She can't anymore," Aurora replied. "That's the difference now. We're not in it. We're not hers."

Isla smiled faintly. "It's sad."

"Yeah," Aurora said. "It is."

They clinked glasses.

To nothing.

To survival.

To the lives they had chosen instead.

The next morning, Vanessa posted another photo.

This one of Graham's old wristwatch, left behind on the kitchen counter like a relic. The caption read like a poem, but it wasn't.

It was a performance.

A girl still screaming for the world to see how wounded she was, how alone she'd been left, how cruel her sisters were.

No one liked the post.

No one ever did, but Vanessa kept posting anymore.

And in a house that still smelled faintly of lemon and dust, with no one left to watch her grieve, Vanessa sat in silence.

The same kind Graham left behind.

Act IV
The Letter She Never Sends

A Letter from Aurora To The Father She Never Had

Dad,

I wish you had loved me enough to stop her. That's the truth I've never spoken aloud—not because I was afraid of it, but because I've always known it would echo. You watched her crush me, day after day, and I waited for your hand on her shoulder, your voice between us. It never came.

I remember how small the house felt. Not in size, but in silence. The way the walls pressed in. The way the air changed when she entered a room. I learned to read the sound of her heels on the floor like a weather forecast. I could hear the storm hours before it arrived.

And you—you were always still. Sitting in your chair. Eyes lowered. Fingers tight around your coffee cup. As if you thought presence was enough. As if your body in a room could be a substitute for protection.

needed you to speak.

I needed you to choose me.

But every time she raised her voice, you raised your eyebrows. Every time she twisted care into something sharp, you exhaled like it wasn't your business. But it was. It was always your business. I was your daughter. I didn't want you to fix it all. I didn't need a hero. I needed a father who looked at the fire and didn't walk around it. Who said, That's my child, and you will not hurt her.

You never said that.

And now I can't remember the sound of your voice except when it was asking for my quiet.

Sometimes I let myself imagine the version of you who did speak up. I imagine him getting between us. I imagine him pulling me aside afterward, kneeling down, saying, *I see you. I know it's hard. I'm here.* I imagine what my life would have looked like if I'd believed I was worth defending.

It's not fair, I know, to hold you against a fantasy. But how else do I mourn what I never had? How else do I hold grief that doesn't come from loss, but from the permanent absence of what should have been offered?

You said you loved me. I believe you thought you did. But love without intervention is cowardice. Love without protection is passive. Love without truth is hollow.

She broke me in ways I didn't understand until I was already grown, already gone. And even then, I found myself turning to you, hoping. For a call. For an apology. For anything. But you kept your silence like it was sacred.

And when I left, you let me go like I was a problem finally solved.

You told people I was difficult. That I'd always been defiant. That I didn't want help. You rewrote me to protect yourself from the reflection. And I understand now that you couldn't bear to face what you'd allowed. So you folded it into fiction and called it memory.

I wonder if you know that I stayed away not because I hated you—but because I couldn't bear to come back and find nothing had changed. Because seeing you sitting in that same chair, with her still in the next room, would have broken me all over again.

There are versions of my life I'll never get to live. In one of them, I come home from school to someone who asks me how I really am, and means it. In one of them, my pain is noticed before it becomes unbearable. In one of them, I believe I am safe because someone stood up and said I deserved to be.

I don't get that version.

But I write to him anyway.

I write to the father I wish I had.

The one who would've carried the groceries and my shame. The one who would've taught me how to drive and how to stand my ground. The one who would've pulled me aside when she called me names and said, *She's wrong. You are not too much. You are not unloveable.*

That father is the one I mourn.

You, I never got to know.

Even now, I try to forgive. Not because you deserve it, but because I deserve peace. I am tired of carrying your weight when you never carried mine. I am tired of trying to fix the story from the outside.

But forgiveness doesn't mean pretending. It doesn't mean silence.

It means saying this.

It means naming what you did, and what you didn't do.

It means letting go of the hope that you'll ever say it for me.

Because you won't.

And this letter, this imagined moment—it's not for you.

It's for the girl I was.

The one who stood in the hallway with tears running silently down her face, waiting for a voice that never came.

It's for her.

Because she mattered.

Even when you acted like she didn't.

I'm not sending this.

You're gone now. And even if you weren't, you wouldn't understand it.

But I need to write it anyway.

So I can finally stop waiting for your voice.

And start trusting mine.

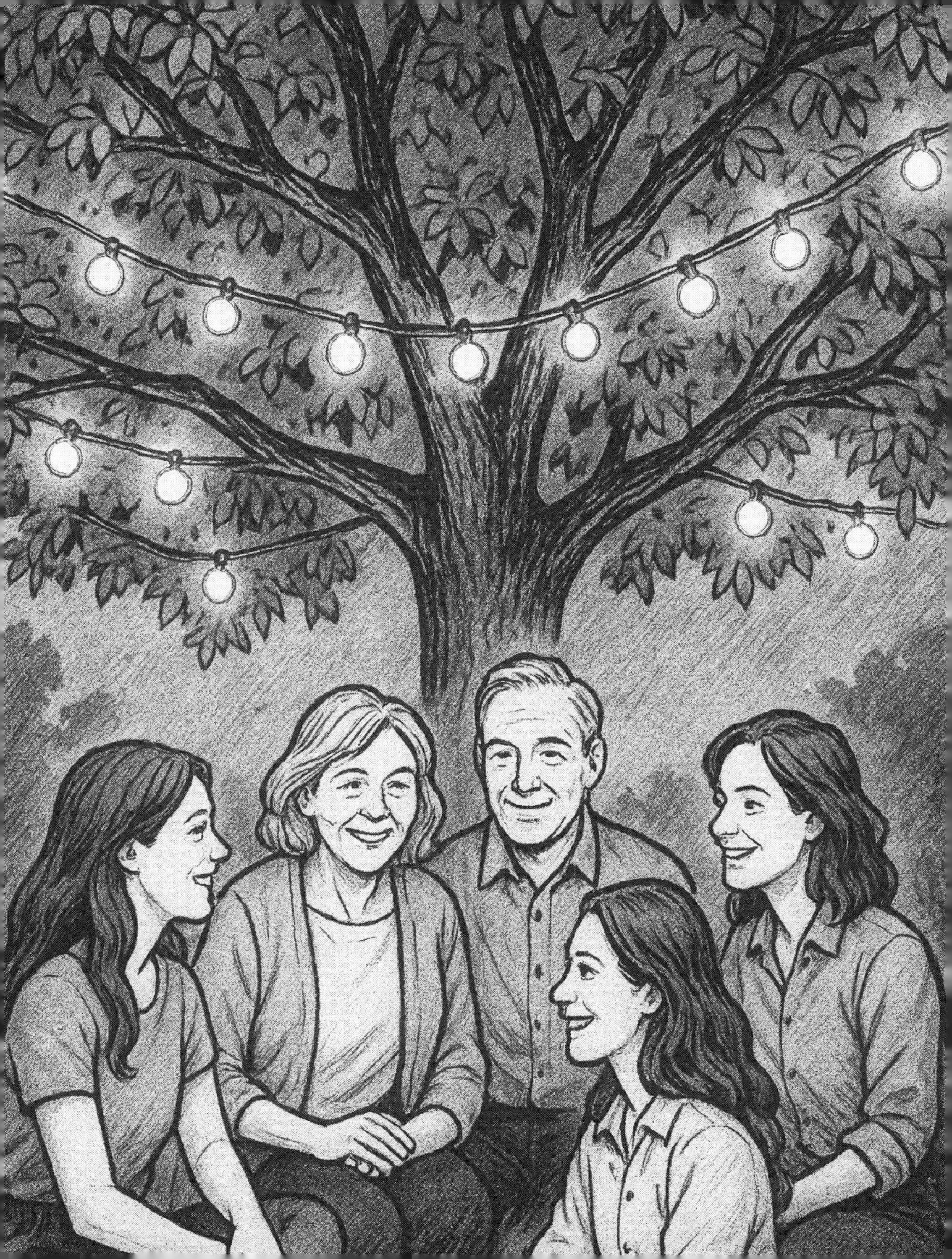

A Final Glimpse Of What Could Have Been

It starts the way dreams always do.

Not with logic.

But with feeling.

Warmth.

Not the kind that comes from sunlight, or fire. But the kind that lives in laughter. In clinking dishes. In the way a body feels when it is seen and loved and wanted exactly as it is.

Isla is standing in the kitchen. The light is golden. Not surreal—not a spotlight or a haze—but warm, ordinary. The kind of light that makes everything feel like it belongs.

She's barefoot on the tile.

The air smells like rosemary.

Aurora is by the sink, humming a song that Isla recognizes but can't name. Vanessa is leaning over the stove, wearing a sweatshirt that doesn't match her usual style. Something borrowed. Something soft. There's a wine glass in her hand and a crooked smile on her face.

There's music playing somewhere.

And then—

Graham laughs.

It is a small thing. Just a soft, delighted sound. But it fills the room in the way only a father's laugh can. He is seated at the table, sleeves rolled to the elbows, a dish towel over his shoulder. His eyes crinkle at the corners. He looks older, but not tired.

He looks happy.

He says her name.

Not as a question.

Not as a reprimand.

Just softly, like a song.

"Isla."

She turns toward him and feels it deep in her chest—that familiar longing, that aching recognition.

He smiles.

"You forgot the candles."

She laughs. "Again?"

Aurora throws her a lighter. Vanessa rolls her eyes but is already lighting the tea lights in the centre of the table.

The table.

It's long and mismatched—plates that don't match, cups with chips, a gravy boat shaped like a cat. There's a roasted chicken in the middle, surrounded by vegetables and a bowl of mashed potatoes so large it must've been Graham's doing, or maybe Deanna's.

Isla takes her seat.

The seat she always used to take.

She looks around.

Aurora's laughing at something Vanessa said. Vanessa's mock-offended, gesturing with her wine glass. Graham is shaking his head, watching them with the kind of joy that asks for nothing. Just this. Just presence.

There is no tension.

No waiting.

No eggshells.

Just the soft, sacred rhythm of belonging.

She feels it in her hands first.

The warmth of the mug. The weight of the moment.

And then she hears her own voice—her laughter.

It is bright and easy, slipping out of her like it was always meant to live in the air, not buried beneath her ribs.

It startles her.

Because she didn't know her voice could sound like that.

Because she didn't know she could still sound like that.

She turns toward Graham again, ready to ask something, to say what she never got to say—

But the light shifts.

Softer.

Quieter.

And she knows.

Even inside the dream, she knows.

It's leaving her.

*****

When she wakes, her pillow is damp.

The light in her room is grey, still folded in early morning.

She's on her side, curled into the blanket like a child.

Her throat aches.

Her chest feels hollow.

But her face is wet.

She touches it, surprised.

Tears.

Not sobbing.

Just... weeping.

The way people do for things they never had, but still mourn like ghosts.

She lies still for a long time.

The dream slips away, slow but sure. Like fog retreating into trees. She holds onto what she can—Aurora's laughter, Vanessa's smirk, Graham's voice saying her name.

It's not the first time she's dreamed that life.

But this time, it felt different.

This time, it felt like goodbye.

She closes her eyes again.

Not to fall back asleep.

But to honour it.

The dream.

The glimpse.

The house that never was, filled with the people they never got to be.

And somewhere, deep inside her, a soft voice speaks.

Let it go.

She breathes in.

And lets it go.

You've Reached The End But...
The Stories Never Stop

Songs To Stories is exactly what it sounds like—short, emotionally devastating, romantically charged, and occasionally unhinged novellas inspired by the one and only Taylor Swift. Because why simply listen to a song when you can spiral into an entire fictional universe about it?

A new novella drops on the 13th of every odd-numbered month, so if you have commitment issues, don't worry—you don't have to wait long for your next dose of heartbreak, longing, and characters making wildly questionable life choices in the name of love.

To keep up with the latest releases, visit BrittWolfe.com—or don't, and risk missing out while the rest of us are already crying over the next one. Your call.

See you at the next emotional wreckage.

About The Author
Britt Wolfe

Britt Wolfe was born in Fort McMurray, Alberta, and now lives in Calgary, where she battles snow, writes stories, and cries over Taylor Swift lyrics like the proud elder Swiftie she is. She loves being part of a fan base that's as passionate as it is melodramatic.

She's married to a smoking hot Australian (her words, but also probably everyone else's), and together they parent two fur-babies: Sophie, the most perfect husky in the universe, and Lena, a mischievous cat who keeps them on their toes—and their furniture in shreds.

When Britt's not writing or re-listening to "All Too Well (10 Minute Version)," she's indulging her love for reading, potatoes in all forms, and the colour green. She's also a huge fan of polar bears, tigers, red pandas, otters, Nile crocodiles, and—because they're underrated—donkeys.

Her life is full of love, laughter, and just enough chaos to keep things interesting.

@the.banality.of.britt

BrittWolfe.com

Manufactured by Amazon.ca
Bolton, ON

45290703R00077